AMY AMYGDALA

By Melissa Reiner, MEd
Illustrations By Gaetano Vicini

For my greatest inspirations and
for my absolute most magnificent blessings,
Eleazar, Ariel, and Shloime,
who from time to time, have been known to
strongly encourage one another to...
"Engage your pre-frontal cortex!
Engage your pre-frontal cortex!"

M.R.

"Don't tell your father how much they cost,"
she said to her nine year old son,
as they stared at the wooden box set of
professional Grumbacker Oil Paints.
It wasn't Christmas. It wasn't even his
birthday. It was his mother's belief in him
and his artistry. One brief moment in time,
that shall never be forgotten. Thank you, Mom...
I love you.

G.V.

Around the time
I was four,

Amy moved in
next door.

We would share a nosh and walk together, exploring the neighborhood through all kinds of weather.

Bria decided to call Lauren a name;
she felt hurt and lashed out
and went kind of insane.

"Imagine I live in the oldest part of the brain,
where logic and reason do not
seem to reign."

"Reacting to stressors,
to fight or to flee-
Amy Amygdala,
it's what they call me."

"If we quiet our brain, release some of the pain,
Amy Amygdala will be calm *again*."

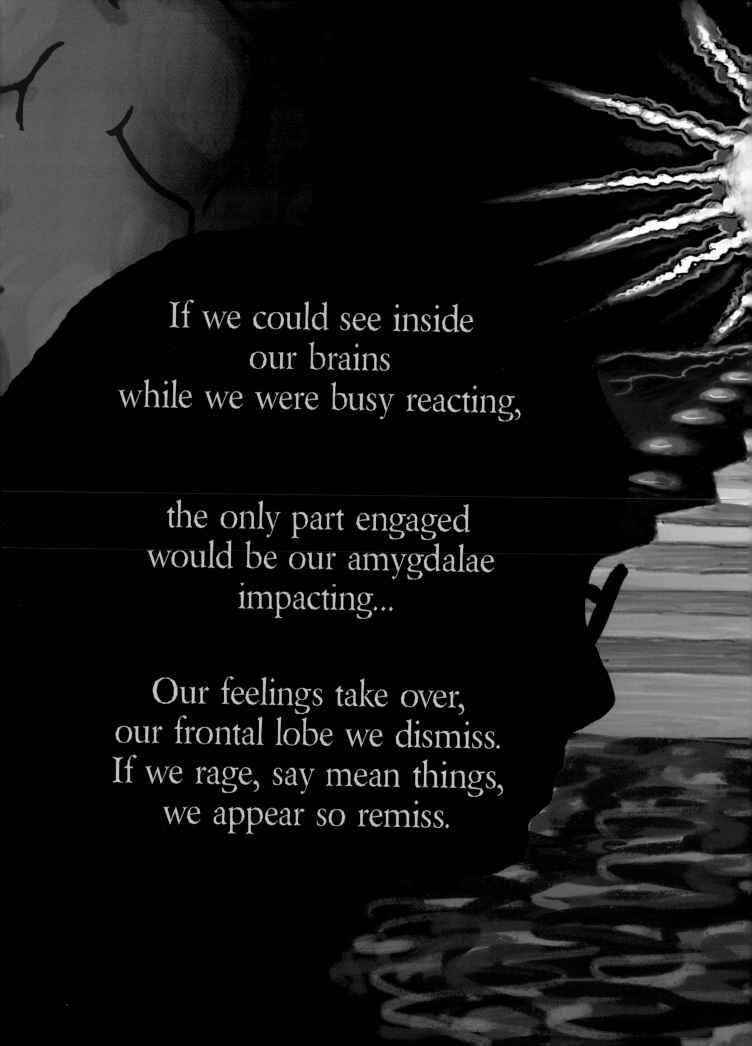

If we could see inside
our brains
while we were busy reacting,

the only part engaged
would be our amygdalae
impacting...

Our feelings take over,
our frontal lobe we dismiss.
If we rage, say mean things,
we appear so remiss.

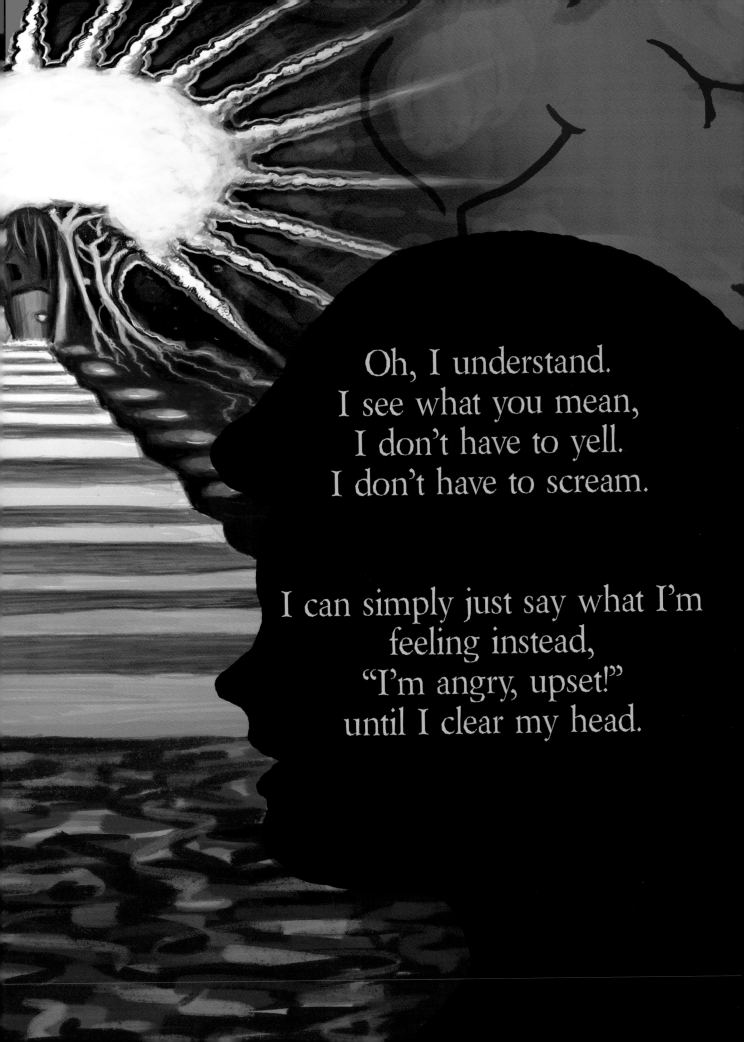

Oh, I understand.
I see what you mean,
I don't have to yell.
I don't have to scream.

I can simply just say what I'm
feeling instead,
"I'm angry, upset!"
until I clear my head.

My amygdalae's job, I understand and I know
it alerts and it saves me from danger and foe.

But if I'm feeling hurt, frustrated or sad,
I won't lose my marbles, I'll just say, "I'm mad!"

That's right! You've got it!
It all seems so clear!

We can tell our Amygdalae
to please have no fear.

THE
END

A special note to parents, teachers and caregivers:
When children become upset, encourage them to identify and articulate their feelings in the moment. It often leads to a conversation that can avert a melt down. The act of identifying and articulating our emotions pulls us out of our amygdala and into our frontal lobe, which is the area of logic and reasoning. Once children can put words to how they feel and why they are upset; then we can begin working towards a solution. If children can learn to respond to their emotions in this way - stating how they feel and why, then reasoning towards a solution - they will begin to feel more competent. The more competent they are, the less frustrated they feel and the less disruptive behaviors will occur.

For example, we might say to our child, "I see that you're upset, but I don't know how you feel." She might respond that she feels sad or angry or frustrated. Then we follow up with, "I wonder what is making you feel (sad, angry, or frustrated)." In this scenario, our child might say that she's angry because a sibling took her toy. At this point, we explore solutions: asking for the toy back, choosing a different toy to play with, finding a way to play with the toy together, or by taking turns with it. Instead of becoming explosive or throwing a tantrum, the child chooses to take purposeful action to solve the issue, which is precisely what builds competence in the child.

Melissa Reiner, MEd

B"H

GLOSSARY

nosh: nosh   /näSH/
informal noun. Yiddish in origin.
1.   a snack, or food.

grappled: grap·ple /ɡrapəl/
verb - past tense: grappled; past participle: grappled -
1.   engage in a close fight or struggle without weapons; wrestle.

lashed: lash   /laSH/
verb - past tense: lashed; past participle: lashed -
1.   attack someone verbally.

feign: feign   /fān/
verb: feign; 3rd person present: feigns; past tense: feigned; past participle: feigned; gerund or present
participle: feigning –
1.   pretend to be affected by (a feeling, state, or injury). "she feigned nervousness."

impacting: im·pact /imˈpakt/
gerund or present participle: impacting -
1.   have a strong effect on someone or something.

remiss: re·miss /rəˈmis/
adjective -
1.   lacking care, careless, thoughtless.

compunction: com·punc·tion   /kəmˈpəNG(k)SH(ə)n/
noun -
1.   a feeling of guilt or moral scruple

Amygdala: a·myg·da·la   /əˈmiɡdələ/
noun - Anatomy. noun: **amygdala**; plural noun: **amygdalae**
1.   a roughly almond-shaped mass of gray matter inside each cerebral hemisphere, involved with the
experiencing of emotions.